Aligay Saves the Stars

Kazuko G. Stone

SCHOLASTIC
HARDCOVER

SCHOLASTIC INC. • New York

To Mr. Mizuhashi
and Dianne

Kazuko G. Stone's technique is watercolor, gouache, and colored
pencil on illustration board. Paints are applied with very small brushes.

Copyright © 1991 by Kazuko G. Stone.

Library of Congress Cataloging-in-Publication Data
Stone, Kazuko G.
Aligay saves the stars / by Kazuko G. Stone.
p.   cm.
Summary: Aligay's star friends help him return home when he becomes lost in space.
ISBN 0-590-44382-8
[1. Stars—Fiction.   2. Lost children—Fiction.   3. Alligators—
Fiction.]   I. Title.
PZ7.S87792Al   1991   90-9148
[E]—dc20   CIP
AC

12 11 10 9 8 7 6 5 4 3 2 1   1 2 3 4 5 6/9
Printed in the U.S.A.   36
First Scholastic printing, November 1991
Designed by Tracy Arnold

One day Aligay made a boomerang. On it, he painted an alligator's face.

As soon as the paint dried, he began playing with his new toy. No matter how high and far he threw it, it always returned.

Aligay played all day and well into the evening. His good friend, Mr. Midnight, warned him, "Don't throw your boomerang too high or you might make the stars dizzy."

Aligay did not listen to what his friend said, but kept right on playing. Just then a big wind swept his spinning boomerang high up into the night sky and out of sight.

Suddenly the sky grew dark. As Aligay waited, four
shooting stars fell down beside him. When he looked up,
he saw a strange blinking object coming closer and closer.

Soon the blinking object landed right in front of him.
"Good evening, Aligay," it said. "I am the space patrol,
and I've come to inform you that your boomerang has
lost its way.

"It is spinning around and around among the stars, making them dizzy. If you don't come right away, all the stars and even the moon will get dizzy and fall from the sky."

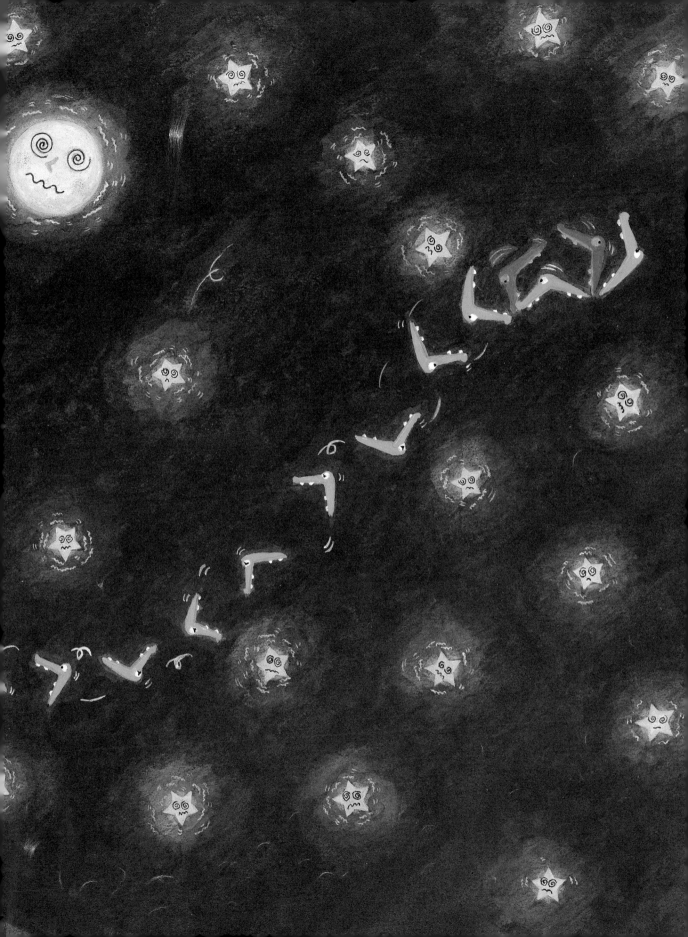

Quickly Aligay jumped on the spaceship. "Be careful," called Mr. Midnight.

"And whatever you do, don't stand up!" warned the space patrol.

"Okay," promised Aligay.

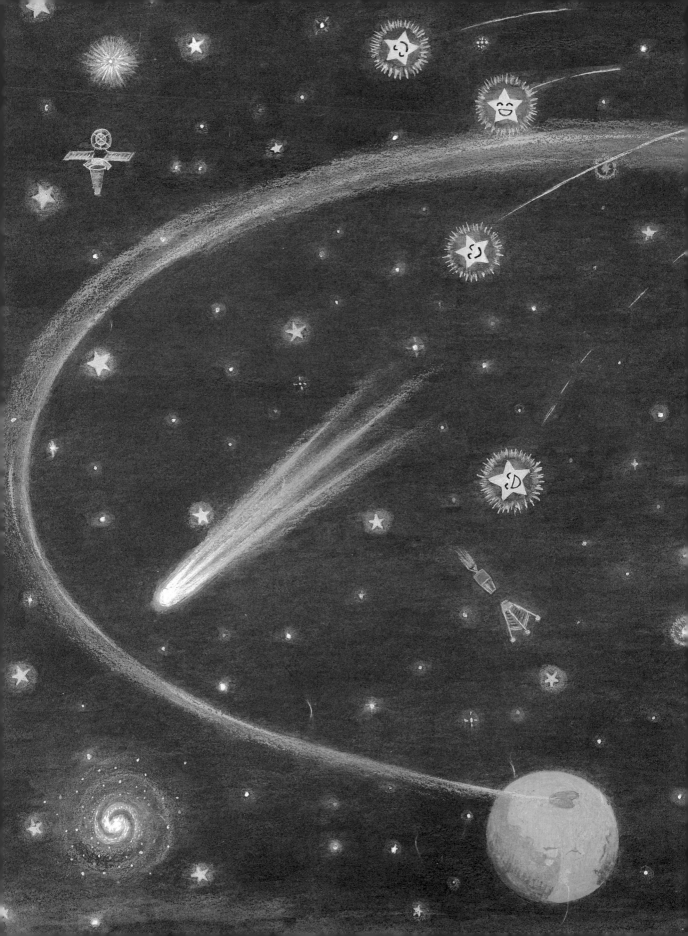

Seconds later, Aligay zoomed across the night sky,
throwing back the four stars that had fallen.
"We thank you, Aligay!" the stars cheered happily.

"Oh, no!" exclaimed Aligay, seeing that the dizzy moon was also falling. "We must catch him quickly!" The space patrol instantly flew over, and Aligay caught the moon.

"Thank you very much, Aligay," said the moon as Aligay put him back up into the sky.

Then Aligay saw his boomerang wandering aimlessly among the stars. "I'm over here!" he shouted.

The boomerang heard him and quickly flew back
towards him. Aligay was so excited that he stood up,
forgetting all about his promise.
  "No!" cried the space patrol.
  But it was too late. At that moment Aligay
lost his balance and...

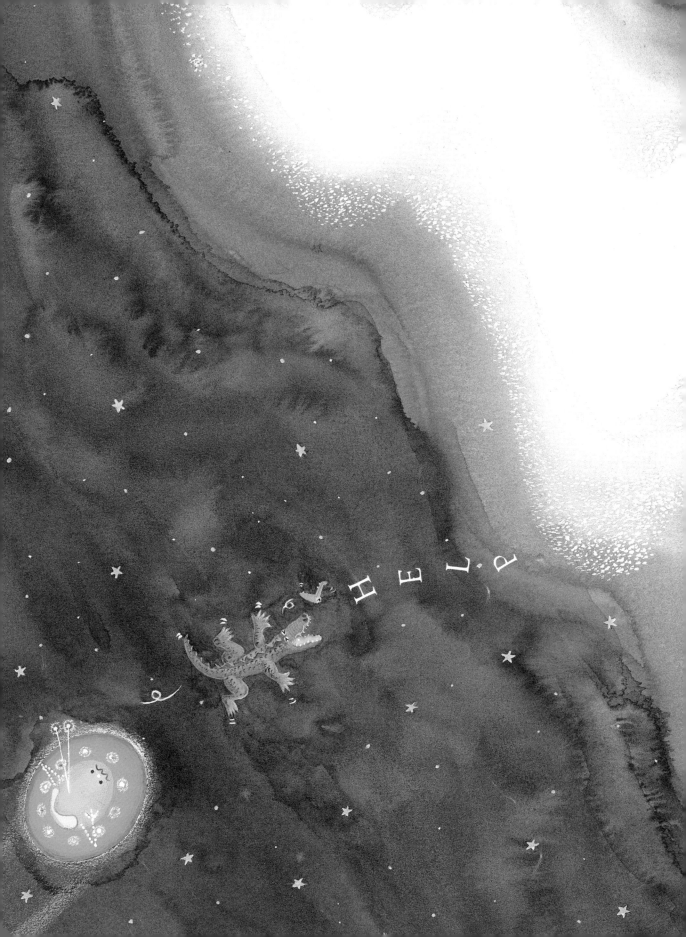

Aligay and his boomerang plunged into the vast,
white Milky Way.

He was a good swimmer and easily swam to Stardust
Beach where the sand looked like stars.

Aligay came out of the Milky Way with the boomerang in his mouth.

"How will I get home from here?" he cried.

Poor Aligay. He was lost and far from his home.

Before long his four star friends zoomed down and sang in a chorus, "Please don't cry, Aligay. You helped us get home. Now we will help you! Come and ride on our shooting star slide, and we will take you back."

Aligay rode on the long, long slide. It was fun!

"Welcome back!" said Mr. Midnight when he saw
Aligay. "I was worried."

"I'm so glad to be home, Mr. Midnight," said Aligay.
"But how can I put my little friends back up into the sky?"

"Use your catapult," suggested Mr. Midnight.

After Aligay and his starry friends exchanged thank
yous, he catapulted each one up into the dawning sky.
And he promised to be more careful the next time he
played with his boomerang.

But now Aligay was very tired
from his big adventure. So he and
his boomerang settled down
together for a long, long nap.